MW01133558

300 Miles

Book 1 in the Perilous Miles Series

P.A. Glaspy

COPYRIGHT 2018

All Rights Reserved

P.A. Glaspy

1st Edition

Published by Glaspy Publishing Inc

Other works by P.A. Glaspy

A Powerless World Series

Before the Power was Gone

When the Power is Gone

When the Peace is Gone

When the Pain is Gone

Chapter 1

Sunday, December 13th

"Boys, I'm home! Are you guys ready to go? We are so, so late." Carly rushed in the door, dropped her purse and briefcase on the dining room table, and headed for her bedroom. She kicked her pumps off into the corner as she was unzipping her skirt. She threw on a T-shirt, a pair of stretchy jeans, and flip flops. *Ah, much better,* she thought as she hurried back the way she had come, pulling her curly brunette hair into a ponytail.

"Coming, Mom!" she heard from the second floor. A moment later, her two teenage sons came thundering down the stairs where she stood waiting at the bottom, purse and keys in hand. One of them a head taller than her already, the other gaining on his older brother, they skidded to a halt in front of her, grinning.

"Let's go, I'm starving! Grandma said she was making lasagna this time. What took you so long, Mom? It's bad enough you had to work on Sunday, but geez, you were gone *all* day!" Aaron, at seventeen, was a handsome, sandy-haired young man who was already six feet tall. He was the spitting image of his dad, but that's where the similarity ended. And he was always hungry. Actually, that was true for both of her growing sons. Cameron was fifteen and looked like her brother, Will. They could go through a hundred dollars' worth of groceries in just a few days. She was constantly stopping at the grocery store on the way home from work for the makings of something for supper or whatever they had texted her they were now out of because the human food disposals that were her children had just eaten the last of whatever it was.

"Sorry, honey, but we're trying to get everything set up in the new accounting system before tax time, plus one of our biggest clients requested a meeting today. You're lucky I got out when I did. I basically told Marcus that either he let me leave to have our regularly scheduled Sunday family dinner or I would quit. He actually hesitated before he told me I could go ahead and go. He can be a dick sometimes."

The boys snickered, and Carly grinned at them. Cameron, her younger son, took on a serious look. "Do you kiss your momma with that mouth?" Aaron guffawed when Carly gave her smart-aleck son the stink eye.

"Watch it, wise guy, unless you want to walk to your grandparents' house. Now, get your butts in the car. Pops will be calling any minute. You know how he hates to eat late."

As if on cue, Carly's cell phone rang. She looked at the screen, then turned it around so the boys could see "Dad" displayed on the caller ID. She tapped the screen as she headed for the kitchen door leading to the garage. "Hi, Dad. We're on our way. Tell Mom she can pull the pan out of the oven."

~~~~~~

After dinner, Carly helped her mother with the dishes while the boys watched football with their grandfather. They looked at each other and grinned at the sound of three voices raised in indignation at a supposed bad call. Looking toward the living room where the chorus came from, Carly could see the lights of her parents' Christmas tree reflecting off the ceiling. The multi-colored display reminded her that she had less than two weeks to get her own tree decorated, finish her shopping, and wrap presents. *Make that start and finish the shopping.* She hadn't gotten to it yet. She had been slammed at work trying to get the system updated before the first of the year. Thankfully, her mother would do all the cooking, so she just had to buy and wrap presents. Her boys had put the tree up for her just the day before, but she liked to do the decorating herself. One more thing to get done. She was so deep in her thoughts at what she still needed to do to prepare for the upcoming holiday, it took her a moment to realize her mother was speaking to her.

"I'm sorry, Mom. What did you say?"

"I said I got the boys new shirts, socks, and jeans, and some gift cards for their iPods. Oh, and I got them each a new winter jacket. Hard to believe it's December when it's almost seventy degrees outside, but Old Man Winter will show up sooner or later. Is there anything else they want or need?"

"No, Mom, that's more than enough. You always go overboard on them; for that matter, on all of us. You shouldn't spend so much."

She dismissed her daughter's comment with a wave of her hand. "Your father and I live quite comfortably on our pensions. Our house is paid for. We don't go anywhere. We don't need anything. We have two kids and two grandkids. What else would we spend it on?"

Carly smiled and shook her head at the woman who had raised her daughter and son to be strong adults, and provided a warm, loving yet disciplined home to them growing up. The gray was becoming more abundant in her hair and the laugh lines more prominent at her eyes. She was thicker at the waist than twenty years ago, and a bad knee kept her from moving as quickly these days; yet she could still work circles around Carly, or so Carly thought anyway.

"Fine, Mom. Whatever makes you happy. Speaking of your kids, is Will coming home for Christmas?"

Her mother's brow furrowed. "I don't know yet. Your brother won't commit, says his work is crazy, they have shows all the way up to the twenty-third, and he probably won't know until the last minute whether he'll be home Christmas Day. Seriously, who goes to a dinner show in Pigeon Forge that close to Christmas?"

"Not everyone has family to spend the holidays with, Mom. There are people who actually go out to eat on Christmas Day. Lots of folks these days don't even celebrate the holidays. When I think about that, it makes me sad for them, and so very glad we do. Do you want me to invite Elliott for Christmas dinner? I'm sure he'll eat canned tuna or something if we don't."

Her mother smiled at her. "Already done. He tried to turn me down, but you know I don't take no for an answer when I want something. He'll be here. He's the boys' grandfather. He's part of our family."

"Why am I not surprised? Thanks, Mom." Carly leaned over and kissed her mother on the cheek. "Let's finish this up so we can see who's winning the game."

Her mother raised a sculpted eyebrow at her. "Do we care?"

~~~~~

Carly Marshall was an almost perfect example of a twenty-first century single mom. She lived in Bartlett, a suburb of Memphis, with her teenage sons, Aaron and Cameron. Their father, Ethan, had left them when the boys were in grade school, and it had been only the three of them for

4

almost ten years. She had a good job as a CPA with a private accounting firm and had been there for six years. She had never remarried, hadn't even dated anyone seriously, instead focused solely on her boys and raising them in a way that they would become productive members of society–good men who understood that good things come to those who work for them.

Her parents, Joel and Lauri Chambers, were very close to Carly and her sons. Joel was a retired mechanical engineer and Lauri was a former high school teacher, also retired. They had very nice pensions which were deposited electronically to their bank each month, half to their checking account and half to a money market account they had had for thirty years. Due to their modest lifestyle, the money market account had over two hundred and fifty thousand dollars in it. When Carly asked them what they were saving it for, her dad replied, "You never know when someone might need some help."

Joel and Lauri had kept the boys two nights a week for over a year while Carly got her CPA. They lived just a couple of miles from Carly, right at the edge of town. They had a mini-farm of sorts, with an acre of land. They had a nice-sized garden that kept them all in fresh veggies all summer long, as well as lots of stuff put up in the freezer for the winter. They also kept chickens for the fresh eggs. The family still had dinner together every Sunday afternoon. Her brother, Will, played bass guitar for a band called Country Forever, and they had a long-term gig at a dinner club in Pigeon Forge. The seven-hour drive back meant he didn't get home much, but he always tried to make it for Thanksgiving or Christmas. He hadn't made it for Thanksgiving that year.

While Ethan had disappeared without so much as a "kiss my ass", his dad, Elliott Marshall, made every effort to stay in his grandsons' lives. The boys spent one weekend a month with him, as well as at least two weeks during the summer, on his farm in Tipton County, the next county just north of them. Growing up deep in the Appalachian Mountains, he had known little of modern conveniences, so he had a wealth of knowledge on how to rough it which he was trying to pass on to the boys. Elliott had taught them how to hunt and fish, as well as some basic survival skills. They could start a fire with twigs and string; construct a primitive shelter; and find food from a variety of sources, including wild edible plants. Elliott had ten acres of land, half of it cleared, with a barn, a couple of sheds, and a three-bedroom cabin he'd built himself years ago. His water came from a well with an electric pump, but there was also a hand pump attached–just in case.

"Just in case of what, Pap?" Cameron had asked when his grandfather showed them how the pitcher pump worked when they were younger.

"In case there's no power."

"Why wouldn't there be power? Oh, you mean like if you forget to pay your electric bill, or something like that, right? You can just go down and pay it at the office, Pap. They'll turn it back on for you." Cameron continued to pump the handle, amazed at the fact that he was actually pulling the water from the ground himself, with his own hands, no faucet involved.

Elliott was shaking his head at his grandson. "No, Cam, I'm talking about if something happened to everybody's power. We'd need to be able to get to the water just like you're doing now if the power was off for a long time–days, weeks, even months. You can't live much past three days without water, son."

Aaron, who had been standing with them through all this, looked at his grandfather like he might be ill. "That's crazy talk, Pap. The power would never be off for months. The longest it's ever been off was a couple of hours. It was so boring, I went and took a nap. When I woke up, it was back on. Even then, the water still worked. I don't think you should be worrying about stuff like that."

Elliott smiled at his grandson, who looked so much like his dad. "Except this water comes from a well that needs electricity to pump it. You never know if or when something might happen, Aaron. There's crazy people all over the world, and some of them have their finger on nukes. We could be attacked. Or what about an earthquake? We're way past due for one. If it hit just right, we could be cut off from the rest of the country with no help able to get to us. Without water, we'd die."

Cameron looked at his grandfather wide-eyed. "But we might not be able to get here either, Pap. What would happen to us? We don't have a well at our house."

Elliott replied, "I'd get you here, Cam. Don't you doubt that for one second. If I had to walk every step of the way, I'd get to you."

Cameron smiled at his grandfather as Aaron laid a hand on the older man's shoulder. "Not to worry, Pap. Nothing like that is going to happen. This is probably the most use that hand pump will ever get."

Elliott looked into the younger version of his son Ethan's eyes. "I hope you're right, son. I really do."

~~~~~

When they got back home after Sunday dinner, leftovers foisted on them by Lauri ("We'll never eat all this, take it home with you") as she did every time, the boys went upstairs to play online while Carly sat down at the dining room table with her cell phone. She kept her lists there, like groceries and to do items, because she always had her phone with her. No making a list and leaving it at the house for her. She connected her Bluetooth keyboard to it and set about making a new list–things that must be done before Christmas. She gazed into the living room at the bare tree, tapped the microphone on her screen, and said out loud, "Decorate the tree." Her smartphone created the line of text, and got it right. Sometimes her Southern accent confused the *smart* part of the phone and she had to correct it from the keyboard. So far, so good.

She continued. "Buy presents for family." Her phone returned *by* instead of *buy*. She fixed it with the keyboard. "Yeah, not that smart," she mumbled as she typed. Her next entry was, "Call Will." The phone handled that one just fine. She intended to call her brother to guilt him into coming home for the holiday. Just then, her phone buzzed and vibrated. She looked at the screen. "Well, speak of the devil," she said aloud, seeing her brother's name on the caller ID. She swiped the screen and replied, "You know, little brother, I've said more than once that I think you're psychic. I just this second made a note to call you. How's everything going up there in Dollyland?"

Will laughed on the other end of the line. "You may be right about that voodoo business, sis. You know sometimes I get these ... I don't know, feelings, premonitions, something. That's one of the reasons I called."

Carly was still thinking about the things she needed to do before the holiday and the end of the year. She half-heartedly replied, "Oh, do tell. Do you see a tall, dark, handsome, rich guy in my future?" Carly laughed. "Seriously, I hope you see yourself coming home for Christmas. Mom is worried you won't be here."

She heard Will sigh over the line. "That woman makes it damn hard to surprise her. Yes, I'll be there. In fact, I'll be home next weekend through the end of the year. The guys are all wiped, me included, and want some serious down time. A couple of weeks at home should be just the ticket. You think that will make her happy?"

Carly squealed. "Oh, Will! Yes, that will make her, Dad, the boys, even me happy! I can't wait!"

At her raised voice, Aaron and Cameron came running down the stairs. "Mom–are you okay? What's going on?" Aaron was looking around the room for anything out of place.

She laughed. "I'm fine, honey. I'm talking to Uncle Will. He's coming home next weekend and staying until New Year's. Say hello." She tapped the button that put the phone in speaker mode.

Both boys chimed in, "Hey, Uncle Will!" Then Cameron added, "You still all about that bass?" Aaron fell on the floor laughing. Carly rolled her eyes.

Will snickered on the other end. "That one never gets old, Cam Man. And, yes, I am. No treble." They could almost hear the lecherous grin over the phone. Cameron held his hand up for his brother to slap. Aaron didn't disappoint.

Then Aaron said, "Bring your b-ball shoes, Unc. You haven't seen me in a year. I think I can take you now. Six feet tall and counting."

"Yes, your mom has told me that you almost have to duck to come into the house now. I'm pretty sure I can still whip your butt though."

Aaron grinned. "We'll see. Gotta go. Grandma's leftover lasagna is calling my name. Later, Uncle Will. See ya next week."

Will groaned. "That's downright cruel. You know how long it's been since I had any of her lasagna?"

Aaron called back over his shoulder. "Duh. At least a year. Why do you think I told you about it?"

As Carly picked the phone up to take it off speaker, Will got out, "Oh, you are so going down, buddy! No mercy!"

The boys laughed on their way to the kitchen. Carly shook her head and put the phone back to her ear. "I swear, sometimes you act the same age as them. But, I'm really glad you're coming home soon, and for longer than overnight this time."

Will got quiet on the other end. "Sis, I'm the one who pushed for the time off. Something is nagging at me, telling me I need to get home. I wish I could head out right now; it's that strong."

Carly sat up straighter. "Then do it, Will. Just come home now. I learned a long time ago to trust your hunches. Screw the gig. Get in the car and go."

"Yeah, but I've had as many bad hunches as good ones. Nah, I'm sure it's nothing, or it can at least wait one more week. I'll head out first thing Sunday morning. I should be there for Sunday dinner. Don't tell Mom and Dad. I want to surprise them."

Carly couldn't hide the concern in her voice. "Okay, but if the feeling gets any stronger, you leave sooner, promise me."

She could hear the smile in his voice. "I will, I promise. Make sure those heathens of yours keep the secret, too. I gotta get off here and get ready for tonight's show. I'll see you next weekend, sis. Love ya!"

"I love you, too, baby brother. Till next weekend then!"

Carly held the phone away from her face and tapped the screen, ending the call, but not the concern she felt. For as long as she could remember Will had gotten *feelings* about things happening, and though he had tried to brush it off on the phone, more often than not something did happen around the time he had the premonition. He all but predicted the broken arm she got playing softball in high school. He begged his dad not to go to work one day because he had a feeling something bad was going to happen. He carried on so that Joel was late leaving the house. When he got to the interstate, traffic was backed up for a mile. He turned on his CB radio and found out an accident had occurred ahead when a car's front tire blew out. The car swerved and spun out, hitting two other cars in the adjoining lanes. When Joel asked over the radio when it had happened, one of the truckers replied, "About five minutes ago. It's here by the Poplar Avenue exit. I saw it happen." Joel's hands began to shake. Had Will not been so distraught, Joel would have been about that far along on his trip to work. He could very easily have been in that exact spot when the tire blew. He never doubted his son's gift again.

Carly tried not to worry, knowing that she would anyway, probably all week. She left the note to call Will as a reminder to check in with him in a day or so. If it was one of his visions, it would get stronger as the time got closer to whatever was going to happen. She leaned her head back, closed her eyes, and crossed her fingers, thinking, p*lease let this one be a miss.* She opened her eyes when she heard the sound of something being dropped in the kitchen. Cameron yelled out, "Sorry, Mom! I'll clean it up!"

She sighed, shook her head, and stood up to go see what had happened. She walked in to see both boys on their knees scooping up the splattered remains of a plate of lasagna. She turned around and walked back out. "Yes, you will. Every last drop."

11

She shuffled into the living room, flopped down on the couch and turned the TV to a silly sitcom. She didn't plan on watching it. She just wanted to rest her eyes a minute before she got started decorating the tree. Within five minutes, she was fast asleep.

Chapter 2

Monday, December 14th

Carly had come in early to try to get some of the final modifications in that had to be uploaded to the software for their firm. She was surprised she'd made it when she did after sleeping on the couch all night. She woke up stiff and sore, but a hot shower worked out the kinks pretty well.

While waiting for one of the mods to finish, she pulled out her tablet and went to Amazon. "Might as well see if I can get some shopping done while I wait, because this is probably the only way it's getting done," she said to no one in particular, since she was alone in her office. She dropped a new Kindle e-reader in her cart for her mom, since she wouldn't get a new one for herself and she was still using one of the original models made. She added a set of fifty classic western movies for her dad, as well as a couple of video games the boys had asked for. She picked out a set of cast iron cookware for Elliott. She knew he'd had his eye on some but wouldn't spend the money to get it for himself. She was thinking hard about what to get her brother, who had every electronic device made, when there was a knock on her door. The door opened and her boss, Marcus Cole, leaned in with a grin.

"Morning, early bird. How's the upgrade coming?"

She gave him a half-hearted smile in return. "Slow. Trying to multi-task and get some Christmas shopping done online while I wait. Have you done yours yet?"

He laughed out loud. "You're joking, right? I'm a guy, a married guy at that. I buy for her. She buys for everybody else. I can do my shopping on Christmas Eve, and usually do. Is there anything I can do to help?"

"Yeah. Give out Christmas bonuses early, so I know what I have to work with."

He smiled wider and stepped into the office with an envelope held out to her. "Damn, you're a mind reader, too. Merry Christmas, Carly."

She took the envelope and said in surprise, "Really? I didn't ... I mean, I was kidding, sort of ... really? Thank you, Marcus!"

"Open it, then thank me," he replied.

She looked at the envelope and back at him. "Is it awesome, or just, you know, it's the thought that counts?"

He laughed out loud. "Open it and see!"

She turned the envelope over to expose the flap and slid a French manicured fingernail under it. As she slid the check out, the stub was the first thing she saw. Gross pay: ten thousand dollars. *Ten thousand dollars! Holy shit!* she thought. Her jaw dropped as she looked at the check, then back to her boss. She had flipped it over to see the net amount. Uncle Sam had taken a stiff payment, but the net was still four figures.

Marcus was grinning at her with his finger against his lips. "Don't scream. You got more than anyone else. We had a really good year and you have been a big part of that, Carly. After we get through tax season, you and I are going to sit down and talk about a partnership. I wanted you to know that all your time and hard work have not gone unnoticed. Again, Merry Christmas, Carly."

"I don't ... I just don't know what to say. Thank you doesn't seem like enough. But, thank you again, for all of it. You don't know what this will mean to me and my boys. I could buy Aaron a car with this. Or maybe pay part of college. A partner? Really?" Carly knew she sounded like a stuttering idiot, but she was in shock.

Marcus was nodding and still grinning. "Yes, a partner, and if you need any help with the rest of that, come talk to me. I've got to get to my desk and respond to a dozen emails. Have a good day." He gave her a thumbs up, turned, and left her office.

Have a good day? This is going to be a great day! She started running things through her head that she could do with the money. The smart thing? Pay down on that one credit card that she just couldn't seem to make any headway on. Or get her dad to help her find a good, reliable car for Aaron. That was probably the more practical thing. *Yes,* she thought, *that is the best use of this little windfall.* Just as she was picking up her phone to call her dad, it buzzed. She looked at the caller ID. It was Elliott. She slid her finger across the screen to accept the call.

"Hey, Elliott. Everything okay?"

"Mornin', Carly girl. Yeah, good out here in the country. How you doin'?" Elliott replied.

"Busy as always. Mom told me you were coming for Christmas dinner."

Elliott chuckled. "Like I had a choice. Look, I was wondering if it would be alright if the boys spent the week with me next week when they're out for the holidays. I could get them Saturday and bring them to your mom's Christmas Eve for dinner. I haven't had them for a week since last summer. I miss those rascals."

Carly laughed. "Of course, you can get them, as long as Aaron can get off work. Did you have anything special planned for this visit?"

"Yep, it's about time those boys learned how to hunt. So, we'll start with bow and gun training, then I'll take them out to the woods to hunt some deer."

Carly paused, concern apparent in her voice. "Elliott, are you sure they're old enough to be handling weapons? Aaron's only seventeen. Cameron is just over fifteen. I'm not sure I'm comfortable with them handling guns. Bows, maybe, but guns? They scare me."

Elliott didn't budge. "Then we need to get you out here for some gun training, too. Ain't nothin' to be scared of and y'all should all know how to use them. Ya never know when ya might need one. Hell, their daddy's been shootin' since he was ten years old. I shoulda already taught 'em since he ain't around, but I knew you weren't into it. It's past time they knew. I'll teach y'all how to use guns and be safe handling them."

Carly bit her tongue to not say anything nasty about Ethan to his father. "I trust you completely, Elliott. If you think the boys should learn to shoot, then I won't argue. We'll talk about me learning later. You want to pick them up or do I need to bring them to you?"

"I'll come get them. Thanks, Carly. This is important. A man needs to know how to use a gun. There's a reason I want to do it before Christmas. If you're okay with it, I want to give them each one of my old guns for Christmas."

Carly couldn't hide the shock. "You're giving them a gun? Oh, Elliott, I don't know about that..."

Elliott interrupted her. "Carly, I ain't gonna be around forever. Their daddy ain't around at all. They need someone to teach them this stuff, and they need to have the tools to use once they learn. And that's what a gun is–a tool. A tool for getting food, or a tool for protection. When I get done with them, they'll know how to use it, how to take care of it, but most of all to respect it. Honestly, I worry about y'all so close to Memphis. Ain't no place truly safe, hell I'm really too close, but there's just so many people there. If something bad happened, y'all would be sittin' ducks."

Carly looked heavenward. *Here we go again. He'll be off on that shit hit the fan survivalist jag if I don't nip this in the bud.* "Okay, Elliott, I need to get off here and get back to work. Just call me later in the week when you know what time you're coming Saturday to pick them up."

"I'll be there by nine. Tell them boys no sleeping in this Christmas break. Pap is comin' to get 'em."

~~~~~

The boys had already eaten by the time Carly got home at eight. After three weeks and the last twelve hours that day in the office, the software update was done, so she was hoping for light days at work the rest of the year. The insanity would start soon after New Year's. She shuffled in the door from the garage to the kitchen. She was beat, mentally and physically. The only upside was that by the time she had left the office, rush hour was over, and her drive home was uneventful and easy. She'd had every intention of decorating the tree the night before and instead had fallen asleep on the couch and slept there all night. When she left that morning, her thoughts again went to the bare tree. *I have to get it done tonight after work.* Now, dragging herself in the house after the equivalent of a day and a half at the office, she dreaded the thought of even seeing it. As she came into the dining room, she could see twinkling lights reflecting in the crystal centerpiece on the table. Rounding the corner, she stood in awe of a fully-decorated Christmas tree in her living room. Her sons were standing beside it, having heard the garage door opener running when she got home, grinning from ear to ear.

"Surprise!" They shouted in unison. One stood on each side of the tree and held their hands up like game show presenters showing off a potential prize. Carly stared at the beautiful results. The multi-colored lights were reflecting off the silver garland and the shiny glass ornaments. Just looking at it, watching the lights go on and off and back on again, made her feel like it really was Christmas time. She went over and pulled both of her sons into her embrace.

"Oh my. Oh, you guys did an awesome job. The tree looks wonderful! Thank you so much."

They stood there for a moment, a family hug in the warm glow of their tree. Then, Cameron ducked out from under his mother's arm. "When you have a slacker mom, sometimes you gotta step up and take control. We still love ya though, slacker mom."

Carly made a move to grab him, but he turned and ran for the stairs. Aaron stood there snickering. Carly called up the stairs, "I'm a slacker mom, huh? Okay, I'll just call Pap back and tell him you aren't interested in going to his place next week and learning how to shoot..."

It only took a moment for Cameron to come bounding back down the stairs. "Really? No kidding, Mom? We're gonna get to shoot? I was just foolin' about that slacker mom stuff. You're the diggity bomb mom ... Mom. When are we going?"

She smiled and said, "First thing Saturday morning. He wants you guys to spend the week with him. He may be headed down one of those *end of the world is coming* roads again, so be prepared. Aaron, can you get off work next week?"

Aaron replied, "Yeah, it shouldn't be a problem to get the time off. Jason will cover for me. I kind of like it when Pap goes down that road. He always teaches us cool stuff– practical, useful stuff you might actually need someday, unlike algebra. Seriously, Mom, how many times have you used algebra since you left high school?"

Carly thought for a minute. "Um, well..."

"See? I bet not once. Did they teach you stuff you needed to live, like how to change a tire, or balance a checkbook, or grow plants you can eat? Nope."

Carly looked at her oldest son. "Do you know how to do those things, honey?"

Aaron grinned at her. "Yep. You taught me the checkbook part. Nana taught me the food growing. Pap taught me the tire changing and more food growing. History, geography, science–that stuff is cool, but food is kind of important, ya know?"

"Yes, food is important," Carly replied laughing. "Look at you, being all adulty." She held her fist out for him to bump. He did, kissed her on the cheek, and headed upstairs to do teenager stuff. She considered telling them about her Christmas bonus, but decided to hold off. She wanted to talk to her parents, and maybe Will, about a car for Aaron, and next week while the boys were with Elliott would be the perfect time to do it. If she could swing it, it would be the ultimate Christmas slash birthday present, since his eighteenth birthday was New Year's Eve. She always tried hard to keep the two separate, as kids born around Christmas sometimes got the shaft and got a combo pack for both at once. A car, however, was worthy of the two, especially since he was turning eighteen. She picked up her cell phone, went to her to do list, hit the microphone and said, "Call Dad about the car." Seeing the text show up correctly, she set the phone back down and went to the kitchen to find a snack.

~~~~~

The North Korean officer stared at the missive he had been handed by his junior lieutenant. He read it three times to make sure he understood.

19

The evil that is the United States cannot be allowed to continue. They flaunt their prosperity in the face of the world. Soon, we will bring them down to the level of third world countries. They will know what it is to suffer, to fight to live. They think we cannot hurt them. They think they know the limits of our missiles, because we have led them to believe we cannot reach them. They will soon find out they have been duped into believing this to be true. We have misled them. Their upcoming Christmas holiday will be one they will not soon forget, because their world will be forever changed. Prepare, comrades. We will show our might very soon.

He looked at the lieutenant. "This is authentic? This is from the supreme leader?"

The junior officer gave a curt nod. "It is, Colonel. Is there a response to send back?"

The colonel shook his head. "No response. We must prepare for war."

20

Chapter 3

Tuesday, December 15th

The weather had finally turned colder. Winter in Tennessee was a daily surprise. It could be forty degrees when you got up in the morning, but you could need the air conditioner on that afternoon. While taking a moment with a cup of coffee before heading to work, Carly checked the weather app on her phone and found that the forecast was for clouds with a chance of rain. Looking at the extended forecast, that pattern was going to last the rest of the week and there was even a chance of a wintry mix coming for the weekend. Carly sighed. Aaron looked up from his toaster pastries.

"Something wrong, Mom?" he asked around a mouthful of strudel.

She shook her head. "No, not really. I thought I might try to do a little shopping this weekend while you guys are with Pap, but it looks like the weather is going to be nasty. I'll try to do as much online as I can. I just hate taking the chance it won't get here in time for Christmas."

"Don't you have that free two-day shipping thing on Amazon? There's plenty of time for that."

"Thankfully, yes," she replied. "I don't know what I would do without it, especially at times like this. I guess I'm in shopping mode today–from my desk." She got up with her coffee cup, stopped to kiss her son on top of the head, and headed to the sink. "Take a jacket. It's cold out and it doesn't look like it's going to warm up any today. Where is your brother? He's going to be late for the bus. Will you go up and get him please?"

Aaron put his toaster strudel down, looked toward the living room and shouted, "Hey Caaaaaaammmmerooooooonnnn! Let's go!"

Carly put the cup down in the sink and placed her hands on her hips. "Really, Aaron? I could have done that. Go up there and see what's taking him so long!"

Aaron huffed, placed both hands on the table to push himself up and grumbled to himself as he headed toward the staircase, "Am I my brother's keeper?"

Carly called after him, "I heard that! And yes, you are!"

Aaron shook his head and took the stairs two at a time. At the top, he turned and stomped to his brother's bedroom door. Finding it closed, he banged with the side of his fist. "Cam! C'mon, man, the bus will be here in like five minutes." He reached for the knob which turned in his hand as the door opened. Cameron slid out and shut the door behind him.

"Yeah, okay, let's go," he said, as he tried to slip past his older brother.

Aaron eyed Cameron suspiciously. "What's going on in there? What are you being so sneaky for?"

"None of your business! Nothing's going on, alright? Let's just go!"

"If nothing's going on, then what is none of my business, punk?"

"It's just ... never mind. We're gonna be late. Let's go."

Aaron reached out to touch his brother's shoulder. "Seriously, what's up?"

Cameron looked at Aaron, then down at the floor. "I was talking to Dad on Facebook."

"What? When did this start? What did he want?" The questions flew out of Aaron's mouth.

"See? This is why I didn't tell you before. I knew you'd make a big deal out of it."

"It *is* a big deal, Cam! He left us. Walked out and left Mom with two little kids. No money. No car. Nothing. If it hadn't been for Nana and Pops, we probably would have starved to death. Do you think he cared? Hell no, because he only cares about himself."

Cameron looked at Aaron pleadingly. "But he's sorry and he misses us, and he wants to be a part of our lives again. He's our dad, Aaron."

Aaron snatched his hand away. "No. He's the sperm donor. He isn't a dad. That title you have to work for and earn. I've heard the stories from Mom about the way he was always trying to do some kind of deal for everything, so he didn't have to actually *work* for a living. He was lazy, selfish, and didn't give a rat's ass what happened to us. He's been gone for ten years. How long have you been talking to him?"

"Just a few weeks. He said he's trying to get his life back together and he really wants to see us. I was thinking about telling him we were going to be at Pap's Saturday, so–"

"No! Hell no! You tell him that, he shows up, Mom finds out, we could lose Pap, too! She'd go ballistic! Don't you dare tell him!"

Now Cameron looked dejected. "Okay, okay! But, what do I tell him when he asks about seeing us again?"

Aaron scrunched up his face, deep in thought. Finally, he said, "Tell him you're not ready to see him yet. Maybe after Christmas. That'll stall him for a while, so I can figure out how to handle this. Don't tell Mom! She's got enough going on right now. Let's go."

They went down the stairs as Carly was calling out to them. "Five minutes until the bus gets here and you haven't had breakfast, Cameron. Here, take a couple of these cereal bars and a bottle of juice. You can eat it on the bus." She handed him the cereal bars and opened the refrigerator for the juice. She scanned the many small ready-made bottles and pulled out an apple juice. She handed that to Cameron as well. She turned to Aaron. "You want anything else, honey?"

Aaron shook his head. "No ma'am, I'm good. We gotta go. Love you, Mom. I've got work after school. Jason will bring me home."

"I love you, too, both of you. Have a great day. See you tonight, hopefully on time for me!"

Both boys waved at her as they went out the front door. When they got to the end of the driveway, Aaron turned to Cameron. "If you talk to him again, you remember what I said. Don't tell him we're going to Pap's. Don't commit to seeing him until after Christmas. Don't say a day, just say after Christmas. Understand?"

Cameron nodded. "Yes. I'm sorry, bro. I didn't think it was a big deal. I mean he's our dad...well, was. I've always wondered what he was like. Haven't you?"

Aaron continued walking. "Well, like I told you, it is a big deal. And no, I didn't wonder. I knew everything I needed to know about him when he walked out and left us. Just let it go for now, okay?"

Cameron kicked a rock on the sidewalk. "Sure, Aaron. Whatever you say."

~~~~~

Unaware of the developing drama on the home front, Carly went to work, and, as expected, it was very quiet. Marcus stopped by to tell her he was taking a long lunch with a college buddy who was in town.

"Depending on how many drinks we have, it could turn into the entire afternoon. You're in charge. You might as well start getting used to picking up my slack." He wiggled his eyebrows up and down and grinned at her.

She laughed and said, "I've been picking up your slack for years. You mean that wasn't part of the job?" She gave him an eyebrow wiggle of her own.

"Ha! Good one! I'm out. Hold down the fort. Get some more shopping done." He waved at her.

She waved him away. "Way ahead of you. Be gone. Have fun!" She picked up her cell phone and called her dad. He answered on the first ring.

"Hey, honey. What's up?"

"Hey, Dad. I need your help with something. I want to buy Aaron a car for Christmas, his birthday, and honestly early graduation. Can you help me find one?"

"Wow, Carly, that's a big deal. Are you looking to finance one?"

"Lord, no! I got a really sweet year-end bonus and I want to use most of it for that."

"Oh, that's great! How sweet? I mean, not that I need to know your business, but I need to know what price range we're going to be in."

She laughed. "Dad, it's okay for you to know my business, especially when I ask for your help. I'm hoping we can find something decent for about five thousand dollars. Is that doable?"

"Nice! Yeah, we should be able to get something decent for that kind of money. I'll start checking on some websites I know of. I'll let you know what I find. How are you gonna do this without him knowing though? If you buy the car, where are you gonna keep it until Christmas?"

"Elliott asked for the boys to come stay with him next week," she replied. "They'll be there Saturday until Christmas Eve. It's going to work out perfect. Although,

I'm a little apprehensive about the reason he wants them this time."

"What do you mean? He's their grandfather. He wants to spend time with his grandsons. I get that."

"No, it's not just that, Dad. He wants to teach them to hunt. To shoot a bow and ... guns. Guns, Dad! They're dangerous!"

Joel sighed. "Now honey, there's nothing to worry about. Guns are only dangerous if you don't know how to use them. Elliott knows what he's doing. Did you know he used to be a firearms instructor when he worked for the sheriff's department?"

"No, I didn't know that. How do you know it?" she asked incredulously.

"We talk a lot during the holiday get-togethers, being the two old guys. I've been out to his place a few times, too. He's a good man. Too bad that son of his didn't follow in his footsteps."

"No shit. Oops, sorry for the potty mouth, Dad. Anyway, if you think they'll be fine I'll try to stop worrying. Let me know what you find on a car. Thanks for your help. I love you, Dad."

He laughed. "Yes, I think they'll be fine. I love you, too. Talk to you soon. Bye, honey."

"Bye, Dad." She ended the call and went back to her shopping, smiling in the knowledge that Aaron's gift would be taken care of. She had no doubt her dad would find a good car.

~~~~~

Carly stopped on the way home and got a bucket of chicken with potatoes and gravy, green beans, and biscuits. Thankfully, it was close to their house, because she had skipped lunch and the smell of fried chicken was driving her nuts. By the time she got home, she was salivating so much she reached up to see if she was drooling. Since she had her purse and briefcase as well, she was overloaded. She honked the horn, which is the universal mom message for, "I need help, get out here." Cameron came into the garage, looked in the front seat, and grabbed the food. He turned and started back toward the kitchen.

"Hi, Mom. How was your day? Do you need me to carry anything else for you?" Carly called after him.

He turned around with a smirk and replied, "Yeah, what you said. Do you?"

She shook her head and motioned for him to go on into the house. She grabbed the rest of her things and followed him in. He was already unpacking the food by the time she got in. She dropped her things in a dining room chair and went straight to her bedroom to change. When she was in comfy clothes, she joined Cameron at the breakfast bar. He had already pulled out plates and put spoons in the vegetables. He also had a piece of chicken and a biscuit on each plate. She smiled at him. "You're a pretty good cook, Cam. Thanks for fixing dinner."

He grinned at her. "Yeah, I got skills. What are you drinking?"

"A Diet Coke is fine."

He went to the fridge and pulled out two cans, one diet, one regular. After adding potatoes and beans to their plates, they sat at the bar and ate. Around a mouthful of food, Cameron asked, "Seriously, how *was* your day, Mom? Quiet like you thought it would be?"

She nodded and chewed. Swallowing, she answered him. "Very quiet. Enjoyable even. How 'bout you? How was school?"

"The same as every day. Boring."

Carly chuckled. "Do you have homework?"

He shrugged. "A little. They take it easy on us the week before the holidays."

"Well, finish it before you do any gaming."

"I will. We've got a boss raid tonight, so I'm gonna go up and get it done. You want help with the dishes?"

She shook her head. "Nah, I'll just rinse them off and stick them in the dishwasher. You go ahead."

Cameron got up and headed for the stairs. He stopped and turned back to his mother. "What are you doing tonight, Mom? TV? Shopping for me?" He waggled his eyebrows up and down with a wicked grin on his face.

"Nope. I'm curling up with a beer and a good book– well, e-book, on my Kindle. Most of my Christmas shopping is done; just have to wait for the stuff to get here so I can wrap it. I love shopping online. It just makes it so easy."

Cameron came back to the kitchen where Carly was finishing rinsing their dishes. "You're done? What'd you get me? You got my Santa list, right?"

Rolling her eyes, Carly replied, "Yes, Cameron, I got your list. You'll have to wait until Christmas to find out if you've been naughty or nice. Get to work, mister."

Strutting toward the stairs, he said to the room, "Nice. All nice. On a scale of one to nice, ninety-nice. Hahahahaha! I crack myself up. Later, gator!"

Carly laughed at his antics as she reached into the fridge for an ice-cold bottle of beer. Twisting the top off and tossing it into the metal recycle bin, she took a long pull, closed her eyes, and relished the tang of the hops on her lips. She walked slowly toward her bedroom, through the darkened living room lit only by the lights of the tree. She loved that look. It made everything seem so ... Christmasy. She grabbed her Kindle and went back to the living room. *I'll read by twinkle lights.* That thought made her smile.

~~~~~

The senior officers of the North Korean military were all in attendance. Every branch was represented. The Chairman stood, causing the murmuring among the staff to cease at once. He looked over those present in the room and addressed them.

"Is there anyone here who did not receive the memo sent yesterday?" Silence. "Good. Then you are all aware of our plan to bring the United States to its knees. To make them understand what it is to not have their nice homes and cars. To watch them try to survive without the modern conveniences they have in abundance. To see them driven so low they will kill each other for food, water, shelter, all the things necessary for survival they take for granted. We will see all this and more in just a few more days."

One of the generals raised a hand. When the Chairman acknowledged him, he asked a question. "How will we achieve all of this, Your Excellency?"

The Chairman smiled. "With one nuclear warhead, detonated high above the center of their country, three hundred miles over the state of Kansas, the center of their land. The blast will create an electromagnetic pulse that will wipe out all of their electronics, all of their new cars, all of their power plants, everything run by computers—everything they rely on for their daily lives. They will immediately become a third world country, with no electricity and no running water, with only old cars able to run. One bomb will destroy their infrastructure which will in turn destroy their country. And we don't even have to leave our homes to do it. This will be a victory for us, comrades. A victory for every independent nation the evil Americans have tried to control with their sanctions and their threats."

The same general replied, "When will this happen, Excellency? The message said their Christmas holiday would be interrupted. Will it be then?"

The Chairman smiled again. "No, we want to disrupt everything before that. We will send the missile early Monday evening. That will be the middle of the night for them. Most of the people won't even know what happened until they rise without their morning coffee brewing automatically. Even then, they won't understand what has happened until it is too late."

Another senior officer, a Navy admiral, spoke up. "How will we get the weapon past their radar? If they shoot it down before it detonates..."

The Chairman clapped his hands together and laughed. "I was hoping one of you was smart enough to figure that part might be a problem. Along with our weapon's range increased secretly, we have also been able to acquire stealth technology from an ally. They will not know about the bomb until it re-enters the Earth's atmosphere over the United States. Then, it won't matter. The warhead will detonate, and their lives will change in that moment. We have waited a long time for our revenge on the West, comrades. The time has come."

A different Army general interjected, "Will we invade then, Excellency? Will we send our troops to America?"

The Chairman shook his head. "No, we won't invade, at least not for a while. We will sit back and watch them devour and destroy each other first. Whoever or whatever is left in six months, maybe even a year, we should be able to easily overthrow and control. Are there any other questions?"

The room grew quiet again. A few men looked at each other, but none spoke. The Chairman stood at attention. "I will personally be handling all aspects of the launch, but I want all of you in attendance to witness this historic event and major coup for our country. I should not have to tell you, but do not discuss this with anyone. Be here Monday morning ready to spend the day watching the preparations for our attack. Dinner will be served in the palace afterward to celebrate our victory."

The officers executed a group bow which the Chairman returned. He walked out of the room, leaving the men to talk amongst themselves again.

"So, this is it? We will finally attack the United States?" asked the admiral of the general who had asked the most questions.

"It would appear that is the case."

"Will it be as easy as His Excellency says? And with no loss of life?"

The general looked him in the eye. "No loss of Korean life–unless they live in America."

Chapter 4

Wednesday, December 16th

Carly took a long lunch so that she could meet her dad in Cordova to look at a car for Aaron. It was a 2002 Honda Civic hatchback, with just under a hundred thousand miles on it. Carly was concerned about the age of the car. Fifteen years is old in car years, especially when you aren't a mechanic, nor personally know one. But the mileage was great and the pics they saw online looked awesome. Plus, the price was right–four thousand dollars. Joel had negotiated the owner down from forty-five hundred.

When she arrived, her dad was already there with the owner, car running, hood up, with both of them under it. From the look of him, the owner was about the same age as her dad. She parked on the street and walked up the driveway to where the men were. The tapping of the heels of her slick-soled loafers got their attention. Her dad smiled at her and took a few steps to meet her as the owner reached in, turned off the ignition, and pulled out the keys.

"Hi, honey. This is Mike Ellis. Mike, this is my daughter, Carly Marshall."

They shook hands. "Very pleased to meet you, Mike."

"You, too, Carly. Well, Joel, what do you think? Wanna take her for a test drive?" He held the keys out to Joel. He took them and looked at Carly.

"You wanna drive it, honey?"

She shook her head. "No, Dad, I want you to, so you can check everything out. I'll ride along though." She turned to Mike. "Mike, do I need to give you my keys to hold for a security deposit while we take it for a spin?"

He looked at her 2013 Ford Explorer and at Joel's 2015 Dodge Ram. He laughed and said, "I don't reckon y'all are gonna steal that little Honda over the nice rides you got there. Go ahead. I'll be here when you get back."

She smiled, dropped her keys in her purse and got in the passenger side as Joel got behind the wheel. He turned the key on, then off, then back on again. He put the car in reverse and listened for anything out of the ordinary. Satisfied, he backed out into the road and headed down the street.

According to Joel, the car was well worth the money they paid for it. It had a few cosmetic blemishes–scratches, dings, and a tear in the carpet in the back–but all in all it was a good, solid car. Mike was more than happy to keep it at his house until they could come back Saturday afternoon to pick it up. Carly was excited about giving the car to Aaron and had decided to use the extra thousand dollars to buy Cameron a really nice gaming computer. Well, as nice as she could get for a grand. When she got back to the office, she went looking for one online. Everything she found that looked decent was going to be two weeks before it would be delivered; definitely after Christmas. Sighing, she went ahead and placed the order and printed the page. She was pretty sure that a description inside a card would be enough to hold him until it got there.

She was very happy with all she had done with her bonus. She was even able to put a couple of thousand dollars into her money market account. That account now held over fifty thousand dollars and was linked electronically to her checking account which usually had a balance of at least ten thousand dollars. Carly was confident that the money in both accounts would get them through most any situation that came up. Her house and car payments were both set up on automatic monthly withdrawals, and her car was almost paid off. She had about fifteen thousand dollars in credit card debt, all of which were also set up on automatic monthly payments. She felt like her finances were in pretty good shape. She had been daydreaming about what her salary and bonuses would be as a partner. It was a really nice dream.

Aaron worked as a busboy as Dominico's Italian Restaurant, just a few miles away from their house in Wolfchase Galleria. Consequently, his family got a great discount when they ate there. He was working that night, so Carly stopped by on her way home to say hi and grab some supper for her and Cameron. Aaron would be fed while he was at work. The owners, Angie Dominico and her husband Tony, were good, hardworking people, who gave back to the community whenever they could, including sending any leftovers to the homeless mission downtown each evening. Angie's face broke out in a huge grin when Carly walked through the door.

"Carly! It's been so long! I thought you didn't like our cooking anymore." She pulled her into a big Italian hug.

Carly returned the hug, then leaned back and raised an eyebrow at her. "Angie, I was just here last week. I'm in here almost every week."

Angie motioned to the bartender, Elena, who handed Carly a glass of water. Elena was also the Dominicos' daughter. Angie put her hands on her ample hips. "Well, it seems longer than that. Maybe you should come in twice a week."

Carly laughed. "Angie, if I ate here anymore than I already do, you'd have to widen the doors, so I could get my big pasta-eating butt through them. Carbs go straight to my ass." She took a sip of the water.

Angie took a step back and turned in a slow circle, hips swaying side to side. "And what's wrong with that? Men like a woman with ... how do the young people say it ... junk in the trunk?"

Carly choked and spit water on the bar. Angie pounded her on the back. Elena laughed and cleaned up the mess. When Carly caught her breath, she replied, "You trying to kill me, Angie? Where do you come up with this stuff? You're crazy, woman!"

Angie snickered. "This is why my Tony loves me. I make him laugh, too. Sometimes choke, but mostly laugh. I'll bring you two specials with extra bread, so you can start packing your trunk." She turned and headed for the kitchen. Elena hadn't stopped laughing. Carly joined her.

After a carb-rich dinner accompanied by a wonderful wine suggested by Angie, Carly lay sprawled out on the couch in sweat pants, moaning. She and Cameron had opted to dine in the living room and watch a TV show while they ate.

"Good Lord, that was good, but oh my God, I'm stuffed! I'm pretty sure the road to hell is paved with pasta."

Cameron was wiping up the final remnants of sauce from his plate with a last bite of bread. He swallowed and added, "Sounds great. Let's eat our way there."

Carly smirked and threw her paper napkin at him. With no weight, it landed in the middle of the floor. Watching it fall, they both laughed at the sight. She leaned back again and held her stomach in her hands. "That's a lot to be eating so close to bedtime. I'll be sorry; I know it. I just love their food."

Cameron burped loudly. "'Scuse me. Yeah, it's good stuff. Maybe we should put that on the menu two nights a week."

Carly shook her head. "No. No way. I wouldn't be able to get through the door in a month."

"Oh please. You're not fat, Mom, not in any way."

"And I'd like to keep it that way. You do your homework?"

"I didn't have any. We won't have any more before the holidays."

She held her plate out to him. "Good. Your turn to clean up."

He took both of their dishes into the kitchen, rinsed them and stuck them in the dishwasher. He came back to the living room, plopped down in a chair, threw his hands up and exclaimed, "Done! Man, doing dishes is hard work. I'm beat!"

Laughing softly, Carly leaned over and grabbed the remote from the coffee table. She clicked through a number of channels, settling on a movie, Red Dawn. It was a remake of an earlier version. The original had Patrick Swayze in it. This one had Chris Hemsworth. She sighed.

"That is one fine-looking man right there," she said dreamily.

Cameron looked at the screen. "Who? Thor? Yeah, he's alright I guess, if you're into that kind of guy."

She replied deadpan, "All women are into that kind of guy."

He got up, stretched and said, "Well, I'll leave you to your lust then. I'm gonna go see how my guild is tonight. Later, Mom."

Carly watched her son go up the stairs. Both of them were growing up, almost grown truth be told. They did their thing, she did hers. She supposed that's how it was with all families now. When she was a teenager, she spent a lot more time with her parents than her sons did with her. But then, there was no internet, not at her house anyway.

Homes with internet access were on dial-up modems, and most services charged by the hour of use. She didn't have a computer at home until her senior year of high school, and she was limited as to what she could do. Now, everything electronic seemed to have Wi-Fi capability, including appliances. She marveled at the amazing advances in technology since she had been her sons' ages and was very happy to be living in such a modern time. She turned her attention back to the movie and let her thoughts wander.

~~~~~

At the same time on the other side of the globe, the Chairman was meeting with his scientists and strategic advisors. He addressed the group. "All I want to know is: will it work?"

One of the young men was nodding his head. "In theory, yes, Excellency, it should work. When the missile re-enters Earth's atmosphere, the heat will destroy the stealth capability, making it visible to their radar. However, the bomb will go off at the same time, so they will not have time to destroy it. The altitude will be perfect for maximum coverage of the country. Any unshielded technology will be destroyed. However, we can't know with absolute certainty whether it will be successful, as it has not been tested. To test it would be to reveal to the United States what our capabilities actually are. However, the test models affirm it should function as anticipated."

The Chairman scowled. "We will only have one chance at this. Once this is done, they will know everything; everything we have kept secret up to now. There won't be another opportunity."

Another scientist, older than the first one, replied, "It will be a success, Excellency. I would stake my reputation on it. No, my life."

The Chairman stared at the man and said, "You already have."

Chapter 5

Thursday, December 17th

Carly's cell phone buzzed and vibrated on her desk. She looked at the caller ID. Will.

"Hey, little brother! Please don't be calling to tell me you're not coming. It will kill Mom, break Dad's heart, and piss me off."

He chuckled over the line. "No, I'm coming. I'm leaving Saturday night, right after our last show. I'll have my car packed and leave straight from the dinner theater. I was just calling to see if there's been anything strange going on at home."

"Strange how?" Carly asked, confused.

"I don't know. I really can't describe the feelings I've been having. It's like something bad is going to happen, but I have no idea what. Usually when I get one of these ... visions, premonitions, whatever the hell they are ... it's about a particular person. This one isn't like that. It's around everybody."

"Everybody in the family? Maybe the turkey will be bad and we're all going to get food poisoning." Carly laughed half-heartedly at her attempt at humor, even though she was getting concerned.

"No, sis. Everybody in the country. It's like whatever this is will affect everybody here. It's getting stronger, too. I see people I don't know, lots of people, sick, hungry, dirty, attacking and fighting each other."

"That doesn't make any sense, Will. Why would the people in our country be fighting amongst themselves? Oh wait, that's already happening. It's just not the whole country. Are you saying the whole country will be at war–with each other?"

Will hesitated a moment. "Yeah, something like that. And everything is dark, like there's no light anymore. This is really bothering me, sis."

"Then come home now. If something that bad is coming, you should be here with your family. Now you're scaring me. Just come home. Please."

"Right. I tell the guys *I gotta go home because I had a vision I don't understand.* Not sure how that would be received, but I know it wouldn't be well. It's only two more days. There's no calendar in the visions, so I have no idea when or if this is really going to happen. But, they do seem to be picking up in intensity and frequency. I get at least one a day, sometimes two. Just do me a favor, and don't ask me why because I don't know the answer. Go to the bank and pull out about five hundred dollars cash. Stash it at home. If nothing happens, you can always put it back in the bank."

Now Carly was really confused. "Cash? No one uses cash anymore. Everything is electronic. Hell, Coke machines take plastic now. What would I need cash for?"

Will sounded exasperated. "I just told you I don't know why, Carly. In the visions there's nothing electrical on. No lights, no machines, nothing. Just do it, please. Do you have that much? I can bring it to you if you don't."

"Good Lord, yes. I got a kick-ass year-end bonus. Okay, if it's that important to you, I'll go to the bank at lunch today. I hate having that much cash. I feel like every thug around knows I have it and is looking to mug me."

"Hopefully, this is a false alarm and you won't need it. Thank you, Car. Does Dad still keep his cash stash?"

Carly laughed. "Oh yeah. One thousand dollars, no more, no less. It may be the same bills he had when we were kids."

"Great," Will said, relief in his voice. "I've got to go. If you don't hear from me again, I'll see you Sunday morning. Can't wait to see the boys."

"Oh, they'll be with Elliott Saturday through Christmas Eve. We could run out there if you want, or I could go get them early."

"Nah, I'll wait until they get back. It will give us some sibling time. I may even spend a night or two at your place."

"Awesome!" Carly cried out. "Popcorn, beer, and corny movies! Okay then, see you Sunday. Love you!"

"Love you, too, Car. Keep your eyes and ears open for anything weird. See ya in a couple of days. Bye!"

Carly placed the phone back on her desk. She really was getting concerned. What could possibly cause the chaos Will described? Some kind of epidemic? And why would it be dark? She pulled up her store list, tapped the microphone button and said, "flashlights." It was added to the list. Then she said, "batteries." Added as well. She thought for a moment, then said, "hand sanitizer," followed by "orange juice." Those would take care of darkness and disease. Feeling better prepared for whatever might become of Will's sixth sense, she picked up her purse and headed to the bank.

When she got home, Carly found a pile of boxes on the kitchen table. She smiled, knowing her Christmas shopping was pretty much done. All that would be left was the wrapping. Addressing the house, she called out, "Mom's home! Is anybody else?" Not waiting for an answer, she picked up a few of the packages and took them into her bedroom, where she dumped them on the bed. She shimmied out of her skirt and pulled on a pair of yoga pants. After exchanging her blouse for a sweatshirt, since she had noticed a slight chill in the house, she grabbed a pair of wool socks and headed back to the dining room for more boxes. She checked the thermostat and found the heat was off. She flipped it on, then reached over the back of the couch to grab the remote and flip the TV to the weather–a TV that was always on whether anyone was watching it or not. The boys came down the stairs and rushed to the table.

Cameron picked up one of the shipping boxes and shook it. "Can we open them? What's in it? Is it for me? I've been a very good boy you know."

Aaron fake coughed as he said, "Bullshit!"

Carly grabbed the box. "Don't shake them! There's electronics in some of these–not for you. Help me carry these into my bedroom please."

Cameron was bouncing around her like a six-year-old. "Can't we have one early, Mom? Pleeeeease?"

"No, you can't. Take the rest of these to my room. Then go get the delivery menu for China Wok. I've been craving their egg rolls."

Aaron had taken a stack of the cartons to her room and was heading for the kitchen. "Hey, Mom, we're getting kinda low on drinks and snacks and stuff."

Carly sighed. "I know. I plan on getting a big grocery run in this weekend after you guys go to Elliott's. Just tough it out until then. We have juice and peanut butter, right?"

He nodded as Cameron came back with the take-out menu. Cameron replied, "Yeah, but that's not snacks, Mom. That's ... you know ... real food. We need junk, the fuel of growing boys. Chips, Cokes, cookies, candy, chocolate. The five C's!"

Aaron looked at his younger brother, shaking his head. "You're an idiot. And chocolate is candy, so it's only four."

Cameron crossed his arms as he stared at his brother. "What about hot chocolate?" he said with a satisfied look on his face.

Aaron rolled his eyes. "Whatever, doofus. Mom, I'll have my usual. Hey, did you hear that?"

He walked over and increased the volume on the TV. The weather spokesperson was saying, "*The National Weather Service has issued a winter weather advisory for West Tennessee beginning late Saturday night and continuing through Monday afternoon. A significant storm system is moving across the Rockies. It has already dumped up to twelve inches of snow in the higher elevations. It's still a bit early to know what the impact will be for our viewing area, as there is an upper level disturbance forming in the Gulf which could greatly impact this storm, but forecasters believe we could receive wintry precipitation of some kind before the system leaves the area. As we get closer to the weekend, we should be able to give you more details. Stay tuned for the most up-to-date weather information here at...*"

Aaron turned the volume back down. He looked at his mother, who shrugged her shoulders. She smiled and said, "You know what it's like in Tennessee. They yell fire and it ends up being a little smoke. I'll believe it when I see it. Besides, you guys will be with Pap. If anybody is ready for a winter storm, it's your grandfather. Now, let's get some food ordered. I need egg rolls!"

~~~~~

The control center was a frenzy of activity. They were closing in on forty-eight hours until launch. The Chairman was pacing one minute, and barking at his underlings the next. He marched into his viewing room and slammed the door. His most senior generals were there, awaiting his orders, if any, lined up like toy soldiers against the wall.

His aide handed him a folder. "The latest projections, Excellency. We are on schedule for detonation at five o'clock Eastern Standard Time, and should get complete coverage of the continental United States, as well as some parts of Canada and Mexico. The only states that will not be affected are Alaska and Hawaii. There is no way to expand the reach that far."

The Chairman waved a hand, as if to shoo away an annoying fly as he read the report. "They are of little consequence. The country cannot be rebuilt from there. Those military bases will be cut off from their command. They pose no threat."

The generals stole glances at each other as they stood at attention in the Chairman's presence. No one spoke, but they seemed to know they were all thinking the same thing.

Are we sure about that?

Chapter 6

Friday, December 18th

Bursting through the office door, juggling her purse, briefcase, and a pricey coffee, Carly exclaimed, "Sorry I'm late! Traffic was awful; there was an eighteen-wheeler jack-knifed on 240. People are such morons when there's an accident."

Marcus nodded as he took her briefcase to help her out. "Yes, Memphis does have some of the worst drivers on the planet, even if the roads are clear, and from what I heard this morning coming in they won't be tomorrow night. Come on down to my office when you get settled. I want to go over a few things with you, since I'm out next week."

"Oh, that's right. You're going to Shelley's parents for the week in Colorado. Hey, I saw they have a big storm right now. You should get some great skiing in." She was shrugging out of her coat as she spoke.

"Yes ma'am, and we are flying out tomorrow morning, so I've got a ton of things to do today. See you in a few minutes." He handed her briefcase back to her and started down the hall.

Carly hurried to her office and dropped everything at her desk. She grabbed her tablet and coffee and headed to Marcus's office. Fridays were casual, so she was wearing jeans and a sweater, which she much preferred over the business attire she was required to wear the rest of the week. The temps had definitely dropped, prompting her to wear the new riding-style boots she had bought herself for her birthday the previous month instead of her usual tennis shoes. Still early for the rest of the staff, it was quiet enough that she could hear her footfalls on the thin industrial-grade carpet. She liked the office when it was like this, before the air was filled with the hum of machinery, the smell of people's lunches being heated in the microwave, and the voices of people chatting amongst themselves in the hallways, talking on phones, or in video conference calls. The door was open, so she went in and sat down across from her boss. He tapped a few keys on his laptop, then turned to her and smiled.

"Okay, I just emailed you my itinerary for my trip and a to do list for the staff. Next week will be dead, deader than this week, so I made a list of some tasks that need to get done before the new year. It's mostly house cleaning, so to speak. Pull the files that are seven years old from short-term storage and get them ready for long-term. Go through the vendors; anybody we haven't used in the last three years, pull and file. Those kinds of things. Everybody can dress casual all next week, so the ladies can wear their Christmas sweaters ... guys too, if they want."

Carly had been pulling up her email on her tablet to follow along and giggled at the thought of some of the guys in the office wearing sweaters with flashing lights or jingle bells. Marcus grinned and continued.

"Yeah, I know what you're thinking. John Harris wearing a Rudolph sweater with a light-up nose is a memory you don't soon forget. So, that's about it. You can call or text me if you need anything. I'm probably going to cut out at lunch today. Shelley gave me my own to do list for the trip last weekend. I should get started on it."

Carly laughed out loud. "Nothing like waiting till the last minute. I'm sure we'll be fine. Like you said, it will be slow, so there shouldn't be any problems. Please stop in and say goodbye before you leave, though. I have something for you, to show my appreciation for the wonderful bonus."

Marcus scowled at her. "You shouldn't have done that. You deserved it, every penny. You want to thank me, wait until you see what your bank account looks like next year after you become a partner. Your life is about to change, Carly. Big time."

She looked down to hide a smile. "I'm so honored, Marcus. I never dreamed I'd get a chance to become a partner. And the gift isn't a big deal. I'll give you a hint: Spanky's Spirits."

"Oh man! I changed my mind ... I'll damn sure take that!" Marcus rubbed his hands together at the knowledge that he knew exactly what the gift was–a big bottle of Fireball whiskey. His weakness for the liquor was well known amongst the entire staff.

With a smirk, Carly stood and gathered her things. "Yeah, that's what I thought. You're very easy to shop for, Boss. Later."

Heading back to her own office, Carly thought about what Marcus had said about her life changing. She wondered exactly what that would look like: a new car, maybe a new house, college funds for the kids, real vacations–her mind spun with the possibilities. Jennifer Russell, the receptionist, was just getting situated at her desk outside of Carly's office. She smiled and said, "Good morning, Carly. You look like you're a million miles away and enjoying the trip."

Carly realized she had a smile as wide as her face, thinking about what her future might hold. "Morning, Jen. Yeah, just thinking about the new year coming up. Lots of changes in the air, I think."

Jennifer cocked her head to one side. "Good changes, I hope."

Carly pushed her office door open with her hip. "Yeah, really good changes."

Aaron had to work that night since he was going to be off the whole next week, so Carly and Cameron went to Five Guy's after she got home from work. There was a line out the door waiting to get in.

"Aw, man, it's gonna take forever to get food in here," Cameron whined. "Maybe we should go somewhere else."

"Where? It's Friday night, Cam. Every place is going to be like this." Carly was checking her email as she spoke.

"Doesn't anybody cook at home anymore? Don't these people have kitchens?" Cameron crossed his arms and glared at the line in front of him.

"We have a kitchen and we are here with 'these people'. Complaining isn't going to make the line any shorter." Carly considered what he had said. "Come to think of it, we haven't cooked at home all week. We've had take-out or delivery every night. How did that happen?"

Cameron shrugged. "One of those weeks, I guess. You're tired after working all day and don't feel like cooking when you get home. I get it. It's cool, Mom."

Carly gave him a small smile. "Well, I'm going to the grocery store tomorrow and I will be buying stuff to cook at home. It's better for you, and I think I'm gaining weight anyway."

Cameron leaned back and looked at Carly's butt. "Yeah, you might be getting a little rounder back there. Not that it's any of my business."

Carly smacked him on the arm. "No, it isn't, buster. Move along, nothing to see here."

Cameron chuckled and moved forward a few steps. "When is Pap coming to get us?"

"Early. If you don't pack tonight, you'll have to get up and do it in the morning. He said he'd be here by nine."

Cameron started counting on his fingers. "Hmm. He'll be here at nine, I need five minutes to sh– er, brush, shower, and shave ... five minutes to pack ... yeah, get me up at eight forty-five, Mom. Plenty of time."

Carly raised an eyebrow. "I don't think so. If you don't pack tonight, you're getting up at seven."

"What? I might as well be getting up to go to school! Gah!" He threw his head back and moaned.

Carly giggled. "You're so pitiful. Go on, we're almost there."

The restaurant was packed, so they ordered their food to go. They took it home, put on comfy clothes, and settled in front of the TV with a movie on demand. When it was done, Cameron went up to pack for his trip while Carly sat down with her phone to make a grocery list. She was shocked when she realized earlier that she had not cooked one meal all week. Everything they had eaten was either grab-and-go, microwaved snacks, or already prepared, as she had recalled earlier. She felt bad when she realized she hadn't dirtied one pot or pan all week. *I'm going to start doing more home-cooked meals,* she thought. *Maybe do a pot roast in the crockpot on Saturday, or a chicken, then we could eat it for a couple of days. Well, I could eat it, maybe Will, since the boys won't be here. All this eating out is definitely making my ass fat.* She added many fresh vegetables and meats to her list, planning to fill the crisper in her fridge and the meat drawer in her freezer the next day.

Aaron came in looking tired and smelling of marinara sauce. He plopped down on the couch and leaned his head back against it, closing his eyes. "Man, what a night. I'm looking forward to being off next week but kinda gonna hate missing out on the pay. I'm saving for a car of some kind, some day."

Carly looked at her oldest son with a smile. "I know, honey, but Pap was adamant about both of you being there for the week. He has ... um ... activities planned for you guys."

Aaron tipped his head up and looked at his mother sideways. "Do tell. What kind of activities, besides target practice?"

Carly closed her lips into a thin line and pretended she was turning a key in a lock. "Nope, can't tell ya, I promised under penalty of death. You'll find out soon enough."

Aaron chuckled as he slowly stood up. He leaned over and kissed Carly on the forehead. "Okay, sneaky mom, I'm going to get a shower and get packed. I'll see you in the morning. Oh, by the way, did you notice they put the brine on the streets? We may get some nasty weather after all."

"Yes, I saw. I still say we won't get anything, maybe a little sleet." She reached up and placed a hand on the side of his face, then went back to her list. "Night, honey. Sweet dreams. I'll get you guys up about eight."

Aaron gave her a thumbs up and went upstairs. Carly turned off the lights, locked the door, and went to her room to spend some time with her tablet and her Kindle before bed.

~~~~~

At the twenty-four-hours-to-launch mark, the control room was buzzing with muted voices and nervous energy. The Chairman was in and out between his office and the outer area, barking at anyone who was unfortunate enough to catch his eye. Most of them avoided him at all costs. If he started toward a work station, there was something on that engineer's screen that suddenly needed his immediate attention. Having run out of people to berate, the Chairman went back into his office and slammed the door. He glared at the members of his senior staff in attendance.

"Are we ready? Is everything set to launch? Are all checklists complete?" He rattled the questions off impatiently, arms crossed, and waited for a response. He didn't wait long.

"Except for the final pre-launch checklist, Excellency. Everything else is completed," replied his chief engineer. "We are on schedule to launch in twenty–" he paused, checking his watch. "–three hours and forty-five minutes."

"Good, good. Now leave me, all of you. I must rest. I don't want to miss one minute of the show tomorrow."

They all bowed as one, then turned to leave. Just as the closest man reached for the doorknob, the Chairman addressed them again.

"The rest of you should get some sleep as well. Tomorrow is a big day, perhaps the biggest day of your lives. We are changing the world, comrades. There will be power shifts, financial twists, and we will finally be hailed as a super power. The one that took down America!"

Chapter 7

Saturday, December 19th

The alarm clock beside her bed went off at seven-thirty. Carly needed a few minutes alone with her coffee before she got the boys up and ready for their grandfather to pick them up. She got up and went to the bathroom, then headed to the kitchen for some caffeine. As she walked into the dining room, she saw she wasn't going to get that alone time. They were both up, dressed, and eating instant oatmeal. She smelled coffee and saw that one of them had popped a pod in the single-serve coffee maker and had it waiting for her. She shuffled over, took the cup in both hands, and inhaled deeply. Leaning against the counter, she closed her eyes and murmured, "Thank you, sweet boy, whichever of you it was who prepared this cup of heaven for your dear mother."

Cameron grinned. "Me! It was me, your baby boy, your favorite son. Your–"

Aaron smacked him on the back of the head. "Quit trying to suck up. It's not gonna get you any more presents, you know."

Cameron rubbed the back of his head. He scowled at his brother and replied, "I've got a better chance of it than someone who smacks their brother in the head for no reason."

Carly shook her head. "This is why I like my time alone with my coffee. It's quiet. The coffee doesn't argue; it just glides smoothly down my throat, infusing itself in my brain. It is non-confrontational. It's just ... coffee and me." She closed her eyes and took another sip as her sons snickered. They grabbed their bowls and took them to the sink. At the sound of them hitting the sink, Carly opened one eye and stared at them. "I know you aren't about to leave those bowls unrinsed so that the oatmeal turns to concrete that I will have to get out later while you're enjoying yourselves with Pap. That's not what you were about to do, right?"

Cameron's eyes got wide. "N-no, ma'am, just setting it down so I can run water in it, and rinse it out, then I'll be putting it right in the dishwasher." He quickly turned the water on and ran it into the bowl. Aaron picked his own back up and grinned at Carly. "Just waiting my turn, Mom."

She headed to the dining table. "That's what I thought. Are you guys ready? Got all your stuff? Toothbrushes, socks, underwear?"

Aaron replied, "I'm good."

"Me too," Cameron added, as he placed his bowl and spoon in the dishwasher.

Carly noticed how dark it was looking out into the back yard. "Hmm. Looks like we might have a storm coming." She set her cup down on the table and went to the living room. Grabbing the remote, she flipped to a local station. The first one she landed on had a weather map on the screen. She turned the volume up.

"A winter storm watch is in effect for all of West Tennessee until Monday morning. Periods of freezing rain, sleet, and snow may be seen in the viewing area. Little to no accumulation is expected, but it could make for some hazardous driving late tonight and early tomorrow morning. Rain will begin this afternoon and continue throughout the evening, changing over to freezing rain and sleet late tonight. Frozen precipitation should start after midnight and last until morning. Lows are expected to be in

the mid-twenties, and it doesn't look like it's going to get above freezing until Monday morning. If you're going to church in the morning you should check the road conditions before you leave. We're definitely looking at our first cold snap, folks."

Aaron and Cameron had joined her in the living room. She turned to them and said, "Grab hats, scarves, and gloves, guys, and your warmest coats. Better safe than sorry. Oh, and insulated boots. I know you're going to be outside."

"You've got it, Mom. We better get upstairs and get our bags. Pap will be here any time. C'mon, Cam." Aaron headed for the stairs, his brother following. Carly went back to the kitchen for another cup of coffee. She didn't get her first cup to herself, but she would have quite a few solitary moments in the next week. She was kind of looking forward to it.

Elliott knocked on the door at exactly nine o'clock. Apparently, the rain had started early, and he was shaking out his umbrella on the wide front porch when Carly opened the door. A blast of cold air hit her, catching her by surprise. She hadn't realized how much the temperature had dropped overnight.

"My goodness, it's getting cold! Come in, and hurry!" she said as he walked through the door. They embraced in a long hug, then pulled away. Elliott took his coat off and hung it on the newel post at the bottom of the stairs. "Would you like a cup of coffee, Elliott? Do you have time?" She then yelled up the stairwell, "Boys! Pap's here!"

"Honey, there's always time for coffee," he replied with a wink. She laughed and hooked her arm through his. As they walked to the kitchen together, they could hear the boys coming down the stairs. Dropping their bags by the front door, they rushed in to see their grandfather, wrapping him a strong hug.

"There's my boys! Ow, careful, I'm an old man; you might break me. You fellas are getting strong!"

Cameron pulled back and looked at his grandfather with a smile. "I'll never be as strong as you, Pap. All that farm living, huh?"

Elliott returned the smile. "You'll be strong as me and more someday, Cam. Let me just sit with your mom for a minute and drink this coffee and we'll get on the road. It's nuts out there already."

Carly handed him the steaming cup. "Really? Are the roads getting bad? I didn't think it was supposed to happen until late tonight. Even then, they aren't talking like it's going to amount to anything."

He took a sip and replied, "No, it ain't the roads. It's all the crazy people trying to get to the store to buy all the bread, milk, and toilet paper up because the weatherman said the S word. The Kroger parking lot was full, and the line for gas was out into the road. Insane, I tell ya. They've only been talking about it for days. Why didn't they go when they said it in the first place? I just don't understand why people in Tennessee lose their minds if they hear the word snow."

Aaron asked, "Did you already go get that stuff, Pap? Running out of toilet paper is kind of a big deal." He laughed as he took a drink of the orange juice bottle he had pulled from the fridge.

Their grandfather chuckled. "Have you ever run out of toilet paper at my house? I've got it stashed everywhere. I make my own bread, get milk from my goat, Flossy, eggs from my girls ... I reckon I'm always ready for a snowstorm."

Carly had a concerned look on her face, which Aaron noticed. "What's wrong, Mom? You look worried about something."

"Well, I was planning to go the grocery store myself this morning, to restock our normal stuff and get some things for cooking here at home. We ate out all last week, and I don't like doing that, not every night anyway. I'm wondering now if I should just wait until the insanity is over."

"Well, we really are out of bread, Mom. And peanut butter and jelly. Oh, and eggs," Cameron said, "and I really think we are about out of toilet paper, since it's the topic of discussion."

Carly sighed. "Well, I guess I'll be braving the insanity then. You guys take your bags out to Pap's truck. We need to talk for a minute."

The boys went over and hugged her. She hugged them back with her standard, "I love you. Be good. Call me in a couple of days."

They replied almost in unison, "Love you, too, Mom! Bye!" then hurried out the door with their bags over their arms and coats over their heads. When they got outside, Carly turned to Elliott. "Elliott, I don't know if you remember my brother, Will, having ... premonitions, I guess is the best term ... about the future."

Elliott nodded. "Sure, I remember. As I recall they're pretty accurate, too. Has he had another one?"

Carly's brow furrowed as she said, "Yes, a few, and it's rather strange and obscure. He said he sees everybody–not just a single person like in the past, but everybody in the vision, including people he doesn't know–fighting each other, sick, dirty, starving, and everything is dark. I don't know what it means, but he's had more than one, that I know of, about the same thing this past week. With no more information than that, I don't know what we can do to prepare for it–whatever *it* is–but we can at least try to keep our eyes open for anything out of the ordinary. I just wanted you to know. Will is coming home this weekend. He's actually leaving about eight or nine, our time, tonight, so if he doesn't stop he'll be here before dawn. He's staying through New Year's Day. He doesn't usually stay that long on the holidays, but he said this one is really strong, and he feels like he needs to be home."

"When I was a boy, my granny had visions. The sight, they called it back then. Almost every one of them came true. She predicted my granddaddy's death; me being a boy, and my twin not living; World War Two, and the Korean and Nam wars. She didn't know what country, just saw our boys fighting foreigners with slanted eyes in different places. I don't discount gifts like that, although them that get 'em don't usually consider it a gift," Elliott replied earnestly. "If anything happens, you get your folks and your brother and get out to my farm. Take the back roads out through Arlington. We can live out there, all of us, for quite a while if we have to. I've got seeds put back for the gardens, there's my meat rabbits, plus wild game on and around the place. It'd be tight living quarters, but I reckon if everything went to hell, we wouldn't be too picky, now would we?"

Carly laughed nervously. "Oh, I don't think anything could happen that would make us have to leave our homes, sweetie. It could just be that this winter storm is going to knock some power lines down or something. Thank you for the offer, Elliott, but I doubt it will be anything that drastic."

Elliott stood up and walked to the sink with his coffee cup. He turned back to her with a solemn expression. "I hope you're right, darlin'. But keep your eyes open and your door locked, especially since you're going to be here alone. Maybe I shouldn't take the boys after all..."

Carly had followed him to the kitchen to deposit her own cup. She figured she'd best get a move on if she wanted to actually get anything at the store. She shook her head at him. "No, no, I'm sure it will all be fine. Will is coming here first, so he'll be with me. Really, you guys go have fun and try not to worry about any of this silliness." She reached out and hugged him. He hugged her back, holding on for a moment longer.

He stepped back and looked her in the eye. "If anything feels wrong, trust your gut and get the hell out. Okay?"

She smiled and nodded back. "I will. I promise. Now get going. You've got some grandsons chomping at the bit to get out to your house."

He kissed her cheek then patted the spot with his calloused hand. "Love you, Carly girl. Call me if you need anything." He headed for the front door.

"I love you, too, Elliott. I won't need anything, but I'll call if I do. Have fun!"

He waved over his shoulder and shut the door behind him. Carly was considering having another cup of coffee anyway when she heard from the porch, "Come lock this door!" She laughed, walked over, and turned the deadbolt. She replied loudly, "Yes, sir! Done, sir!" She peeked out the front window and watched as they left. With a sigh, she changed her mind again about the coffee and headed to her bedroom to get dressed to go to the store. "Well, this is just going to suck big time," she said out loud to her now empty house, "so I might as well get it over with."

The grocery store was insane. There were no parking spaces. Cars were pulled up onto the median strips, in the steakhouse parking lot next door, and a couple were arguing with a tow truck driver who had loaded their car up because they had parked illegally in the fire zone. People were lined up to get grocery carts because there were none. Some people were following others who were leaving out into the parking lot to get their cart when they were finished loading their cars. Some were even nice enough to help them load their cars, so they could get their hands on the carts faster. The drizzly rain just made it all more miserable.

Carly lucked out and got a parking space at the very end of the lot. As she was making the long walk to the doors beneath her umbrella, she wished she had chosen the flat fleece-lined boots she had pulled out of her closet first over the chunky-heeled ones she decided to wear. Stylish yes, but not really the boots you want to be wearing when you're on your feet on concrete for a few hours. And it was looking like that was how this trip was going to go. She found an abandoned cart in the grass strip. Thinking it was her lucky day, she grabbed it by the handle to pull it toward her ... but it didn't budge. Looking down, she found one of the front wheels turned in at an odd angle. The cart had apparently been hit by a car and was no longer functional. Dejectedly, she headed for the store.

When she got inside, it was worse than the parking lot. People were grabbing things off shelves that someone else was in the process of reaching for; a woman passed her with a cart that had at least ten loaves of bread. *What the hell is she going to do with all that bread?* Carly thought as she collapsed her wet umbrella and stuck it inside one of the courtesy bags by the door. Heading straight for the bread aisle, she found just a couple of loaves of some specialty breads, a few packs of bagels and English muffins, and some raisin bread. She grabbed one of the loaves of bread and a pack of bagels. Some lady tried to get the bagels before her. Carly snatched them up and stared at the woman.

"Well, ex-*cuse* me!" the woman said indignantly. "I saw you already had one of the last loaves of bread. I didn't know you were going to take *everything* that's left."

Carly spied the other woman with the cart full of bread and pointed at her. "I didn't. She did." She turned away and headed for the peanut butter. She heard the two women arguing as she went down the aisle.

The peanut butter and jelly section wasn't quite as bad as the bread, so she picked up some of each. She was already starting to feel like a juggler in the circus, but there were still no unused carts around. Scanning the store, she found a display of coolers. She picked the biggest one that had a handle and wheels. Feeling proud of herself, she continued on her quest, checking her list for other things she could pick up quickly. The big grocery trip she had planned was being altered to one that would get her through the next couple of days instead. She could barely get down the aisles for the people filling them. The flashlight and battery shelves were empty. She grabbed some of the pricier tuna, which was all that was left, and a couple of cans of some obscure soup she'd never had before, but the picture looked good, and again, it was all that was left. She was able to grab a large dispenser of hand sanitizer. *Well, one thing off my list at least.*

When she got to the paper products, she wasn't surprised to find that most of the toilet paper was gone. There were very few, very generic, one-ply single rolls, what her dad called John Wayne toilet paper. "It's rough and tough and doesn't take shit off anybody," he'd say with a laugh. She picked one up and put it in her cooler. Then, remembering Will was coming in, she picked up another, as well as a couple of boxes of tissues and two rolls of paper towels. A young man saw her depositing her items inside the cooler and commented on it.

"Hey! That's pretty smart! Where'd you get that cooler, ma'am?"

Carly smiled at the first polite person she had encountered in the store. "Thank you. Yes, there were a few different sizes two aisles over. Hopefully there's still some left."

"Thanks! You rock!" he remarked as he headed that way at a jog. She grinned to herself and continued on.

At the dairy case, there was only the most expensive, free-range, organic, brown eggs left. She took a dozen. She found a half-gallon of skim milk, which she personally thought was like drinking milk water, but still, it was better than nothing. She impulsively grabbed a pack of sliced cheese, because grilled cheese sandwiches sounded good right then. She picked up a tub of margarine, too.

Squeezing through the people who were standing in line to check out, she had one more stop to make, the beer aisle. While the stock was lower than normal, there was still quite a bit to choose from. She grabbed a case of Michelob Ultra to placate herself on the thoughts she was getting fat. Will would just have to deal with it. As she turned to find a place in line, she spied the nuts, placed conveniently across from the beer. She picked out a large container of dry-roasted peanuts and another of cashews. *Okay, I guess I'm hungry. I need to get out of here before I'm the proud owner of the salty snacks aisle.* She chuckled to herself as she made her way to the front.

For all the insanity and rudeness within the store, the checkout lines were long, but not as frantic. Apparently, everyone having gotten their hands on the supplies they wanted made them calmer and nicer. The cashiers looked harried, but they were checking people out as fast as they could. Carly stood patiently waiting her turn, munching on the nuts. The drink cooler beside her was empty except for some ridiculously priced water. She took one anyway. A woman behind her tapped her on the shoulder. Carly turned, and the woman smiled at her.

"Ingenious idea, with the cooler. Were you the one that started it?"

Carly shrugged. "I don't know. What do you mean, started it?"

The stranger was holding a laundry basket full of her own buys. "I saw a young man with one and he said he saw a lady do it and that's where he got the idea. By the time I got to the aisle they were all gone, but it gave me the idea to find an alternate basket." She indicated the basket in her hands. "I needed a new one anyway."

Carly laughed. "To tell you the truth, I've been wanting one of these big rolling coolers to use out on the patio. And it was on sale!"

They talked as they waited, the line moving slowly but moving. When Carly finally got to the register, she placed the cooler on the conveyor belt, along with her other items. The cashier, whose name tag read "Lauren", looked at her somewhat confused.

"You want the cooler, too?"

"Sure. I used it as a cart, but I can use it at home, too. Is that okay?" Carly asked.

The young girl gave her a small smile. "You're the first one who bought the cooler they used." She pointed to the wall at the front of the store and saw rolling coolers in all sizes and configurations lined up. "Everyone else said they didn't need it."

It hadn't occurred to Carly not to buy it after she used it. It just didn't seem right to her. "Well, I do need it. Ring it up please."

Lauren told her the total. Carly pulled out a credit card and slid it through the card reader. She typed in her pin and was handed her receipt. She smiled at the cashier. "Thank you. Please try to have a good day, hun."

Smiling in return, Lauren replied, "Yes, ma'am, I'll sure try. You have a good day, too!"

Carly walked to her car rolling the full cooler–so full she couldn't close the lid–and carrying the case of beer in her other hand. Her hands were full so her umbrella was sitting uselessly in her purse. At least she had a hood on the raincoat she had chosen to wear. She got a few glances from people in the parking lot looking around for available shopping carts, who then smiled at her or gave her a thumbs up, and hurried into the store to find their own. She grinned and walked a bit taller. To no one in particular, she said, "Carly Marshall. Problem solver."

By the time she got home and put everything away, it was past lunchtime. She made the grilled cheese sandwiches and turned the gas logs on in the fireplace. The temperature was definitely dropping, and it was really starting to feel like Christmas. She turned the TV to a digital music channel playing Christmas music and pulled out wrapping paper to start wrapping presents. Her phone dinged that she had received a text message. She picked it up and saw that it was from Will.

Heading out right after the show tonight. Leaving from the dinner theater. Nine my time. I'm planning to drive straight through, so I should be there by three your time as long as this weather coming in doesn't screw me up. Coming to your place. I have the key you gave me so don't wait up. If I don't wake you up, I'll crash on the couch when I get there. See ya tomorrow morning, sis.

63

Carly smiled at the phone. She tapped the microphone and replied, "Go on up to Aaron's room when you get here. I'll put fresh sheets on the bed. Can't wait to see you. Drive safe, Will." The phone got most of it right. She fixed a couple of things then hit the arrow to send the message. He sent her back a sticker of a guy with a guitar and his thumb raised. She set the phone down and went back to her present wrapping.

About an hour later, her dad called. "Hey, honey. I was thinking we might ought to go ahead and pick up Aaron's car today. I don't like the nasty weather they're calling for. I checked with Mike and he's home. Can you go now? I can pick you up then follow you back home."

"Sure, Dad. That's a really good idea. I hadn't even thought about it, to be honest. I'll be ready by the time you get here." She hung up and went to get some flatter-heeled boots than she had worn to the grocery store.

They picked up the car and brought it back to her house. With her dad's help, they put Aaron's car in the garage and left Carly's in the driveway. The second slot of her two-car garage was full of bikes, gardening tools (though she wasn't much of a gardener), mulch that never got put down in the flower beds, and assorted stuff that a family accumulates and doesn't use a lot ... or stops using and doesn't get rid of. Looking at the piles of unused items, Carly sighed. *I really need to go through this stuff and get rid of the crap we don't need, especially now that we are going to be a two-car family. Maybe I can work on that this week while the boys are gone. I might even be able to get Will to help me.* She hit the button to close the garage door and went inside.

After a solitary supper of soup and another grilled cheese, she read for a while, curled up on the sofa with a blanket and a beer. The TV was on with the volume down low, but she wasn't paying attention to it until the emergency siren sound started coming from it. She looked up and saw the banner scrolling across the bottom of the screen and the weatherman on at a time that wasn't scheduled. She turned the volume up.

"...the latest development in the storm headed our way. There appears to be a strong chance that we could receive a significant accumulation of ice as the temperatures dip below freezing tonight. The system has stalled and slowed but we are still expecting frozen precipitation in the form of sleet, freezing rain, and possibly snow. We are seeing rain in our area now. The National Weather Service has issued a winter storm warning for the entire state of Tennessee, as well as the northern half of Mississippi and Alabama. Travel is expected to be extremely hazardous in the morning. We will update you again as this system becomes firmly established in our area."

Carly got up and went to the front window. She could see that it had started sleeting, but she hadn't heard it. Unless it was blowing sideways she usually didn't. With a full floor above her, as well as an attic, she couldn't hear it hitting the roof; although if it rained hard enough she could hear it in the fireplace flue. It all just looked wet outside. She let the curtain go and checked the temp on the weather app on her phone. Thirty-five degrees. Not freezing yet, even though there was sleet falling. Just then, she got another text from Will.

Heading out now. See ya in a few hours.

She sent back, *they're saying it's going to get bad. Please be careful. Pull over if it gets too dangerous.*

He replied, *I'm in a four-wheel drive SUV, sis. I can handle it. Don't worry. Love ya.*

Love you, too. See you soon. She pushed the sleep button on her phone and watched the screen go dark.

With a yawn, she checked the doors to make sure they were locked, turned off the gas logs, and went to bed, even though it was only a little after eight. After the day she'd had, she was worn out. No way she could make it to wait for Will to get there. She'd see him in the morning.

Chapter 8

Sunday, December 20th, 2:00 AM Central Standard Time

Will was making pretty good time. The upside to driving at night was there were fewer cars on the road. The insanity that was Pigeon Forge and Sevierville traffic on the weekend slowed him down a bit getting out of town, but once he hit I-40 it was much better. Getting through Knoxville and Nashville was pretty smooth.

After two shows he should have been wiped out, but the premonitions were so strong that he was wide awake and anxious to get home. He had stopped at the North Forty Truck Stop just after crossing the Tennessee River to stretch his legs, gas up, and grab a burger. He checked the weather on his phone since he had run into the rain and thought there might have been some sleet mixed into what was hitting the windshield. The temperature was thirty-two at his current location. He looked up at the television screen mounted on the wall in front of him and saw that it was showing a weather update as well. Memphis and the surrounding area were showing covered in pink–ice. *Great. That should make for shitty driving conditions.*

He got a large coffee to go and went to pay his bill. He overheard a couple of truckers at a table he passed.

"Memphis is getting bad from what I heard over the radio. They say the roads are getting slick, even with the brine down. Glad I'm going the other way."

"Wish I was. That's where my load is going," his companion replied.

"Stay safe, brother. Pull off if you have to. Ain't no delivery worth losing your truck or your life over."

"Amen to that."

Will continued on to the register contemplating what could become a tense drive. The woman behind the counter smiled and asked, "Was everything alright, sir?"

Will nodded as he handed her the tab and a credit card. "Yes, it was. It always is. I don't get through here too often but when I do, I always stop for a burger and onion rings. Y'all got it going on with that one."

She laughed, "Why thank you! I'll pass that on to the kitchen staff. Anything else we can do for you?"

"Nope, I don't guess so, unless you can magic away this weather I'm apparently driving into."

She frowned. "I wish I could. A few of our regulars said it's getting nasty out there. You be careful now." She handed him his card and a receipt.

"Yes ma'am, I intend to. Night." He headed for the door.

"Night and have a good evening!" she called after him.

He stopped at the door and looked back. "That's probably not gonna happen." He chuckled, waved at her, and went out the door. Heading to his car, he felt sleet hitting his face and hands. As he put his key in the ignition, he said aloud, "Definitely not gonna happen."

Even with the frozen precipitation falling, the interstate was relatively clear. The big trucks that were the majority of the traffic at that time of night were good for providing the heat to keep it slushy, at least. Although the sense of urgency he felt to get home was still strong, he had slowed down to make sure he could control the car if he hit a solid spot. He had just crossed the Fayette County line, which meant he was less than an hour from home, as long as the roads didn't get any worse. He was feeling a sense of relief when the vision hit. He quickly pulled off onto the shoulder.

As many times before, everything was dark. It looked like it was nighttime, but there were no lights at all. He was seeing a street that clearly had streetlights, but they weren't on. Cars were sitting in the middle of the road seemingly abandoned by their owners. It was eerily quiet, no sounds from cars, planes, nothing. There were fires burning in trashcans with people standing around them. They looked like homeless people, with dirty, torn clothes, and greasy hair, but they were in a driveway in a suburban neighborhood, not some alley downtown. They were roasting and eating what looked like a small furry creature as if were the best steak ever made. It very much resembled a rat.

Houses had boarded-up windows as if they were abandoned or condemned, but there were clearly tendrils of smoke coming out of the chimneys. Darkened porches, upon closer inspection, held men and women with long rifles and shotguns in view, seeming to be sending a message to stay away. The sound of a small child crying was cut off abruptly, replaced by the low whine of a dog. The dog ambled slowly into view, its ribs showing through its mangy fur. Apparently looking for food, and drawn by the smell of the roasting rodent, it approached the people at the barrel who threw stones at it to drive it away. They then went back to eating their meat.

A few feet away from the garbage can fire group lay an old man. He was clad in only a sleeveless T-shirt and boxer shorts, even though it was apparent it was cold out, since the other people's breath could be seen. He lay in a fetal position, shivering and moaning. He looked as if he had been beaten and left for dead and hadn't eaten in weeks. No one went to help him. None of them acted like they even knew he was there.

Suddenly, the sound of a motorized vehicle could be heard, then more than one. Into the scene came several older cars and trucks. They held men and women of all types, all races, all ages–and all heavily armed. The barrel people disappeared into the darkness. The vehicles stopped, and everyone got out of them. A couple sauntered over to the old man lying on the ground. They pointed and laughed at him, kicked him, then one of the men drove the butt of his rifle into the old man's face. The moaning and shivering stopped. They turned to walk away, still laughing.

The vision ceased, and Will was left with a cold chill at the violent end met by an old man he didn't know. He still didn't understand what he was seeing but he had a strong sense that it was something that was going to happen. There had been too many visions, too frequently, all with the same theme for it not to come to pass. He looked at the clock on the dash. Two-thirty. He had changed it from Eastern Time to Central at the truck stop. He'd lost some time by stopping when the vision came, but he didn't want to wreck since the visions had a way of taking over his sight so that he couldn't see anything but what was playing out in his mind. He didn't want to miss anything in it either, hoping it might give him a clue as to what happened, when, or why. It hadn't given him any of those things. The one thing it did give him was fear of what was to come. He pulled back onto the highway and headed for home, the pull to get there stronger than ever.

~~~~

"... four, three, two, one, launch!"

The control room was silent but for the lone voice counting down to the firing of the missile. The silence continued as the screens around the room all showed the same thing: a missile lifting off, heading in an arcing pattern toward the upper atmosphere. The young woman monitoring the radar screen was next to speak.

"No signs of the missile on radar, Excellency. The stealth shield is holding as expected."

The Chairman stood with his hands clasped behind his back and surveyed the room. All eyes were on him, waiting for his reaction to the news of a successful launch. He nodded. Addressing the room, he replied, "Today is a day that will forever change the world. Today the small country of North Korea has brought the United States to its knees. Put the large display on their news network CNN. Put the one beside it on Fox News. On the other side, MSNBC. Watch as it all goes dark. We will celebrate our victory once it is confirmed."

The monitors were changed immediately. All eyes were glued to them as the same lone voice announced the time lapse.

"Launch plus five minutes." "Launch plus ten minutes." "Launch plus twenty minutes." "The missile will re-enter the atmosphere in four, three, two, one, mark!"

"Stealth is down!" reported another tech. "The nuclear ordinance has been deployed. We have detonation!"

All eyes were glued to the screens at the front of the room. Nothing out of the ordinary. All reporting on another scandal by another politician. They didn't know about the attack yet. Then, as one, the screens went to static. The Chairman clapped his hands.

"Victory, comrades! We have sent them back one hundred and fifty years technologically. Now, we will watch as they devour themselves from within. This will be one of our greatest days in history–the day we reduced the evil West to a memory of its former self. All of you are a part of that now! Let us celebrate!"

A cheer rose from the occupants of the control room. The tiny country known as North Korea had effectively killed the lifestyles of the people of the continental United States. Most of them, sleeping soundly in their beds, didn't yet know that anything was different. But they would. Soon, they would all know that their world had changed forever.

Excerpt from Book 2 in the Perilous Miles Series, 15 Miles from Home

Chapter 1

Sunday, December 20th - The White House

5:00 AM Eastern Standard Time

President Barton Olstein was awake, though still in bed. He was going over his speech for the press conference coming up that morning; another attempt to assure the American people that the economy was strong, even as the national debt soared to epic proportions. He had marked out comments he felt made him look weak, or as if he wasn't doing everything he could to make the situation better. He was finishing up the last of the changes he wanted made when the sky outside lit up like daylight had come all at once. He watched the display, mesmerized. After a few moments, the light faded outside as the lights went off inside. Secret Service Agent Walters burst through the door.

"Mr. President, we have to get you to the bunker. Now!"

The President jumped out of bed. "What's going on?"

Agent Walters was grabbing clothes off the settee at the foot of the bed. "We don't know, sir, but all the power is out."

"In the city?" the President asked.

"As far as we can tell, sir, everywhere."

"What do you mean everywhere? The entire country? That's impossible!" the President replied, indignantly.

"Sir, we can discuss this further once you are secure. We have to go now. Come with me please." Walters had shoved clothes, shoes, and an overcoat into a duffel bag which he slung over his shoulder. He firmly grasped the President's arm and started to usher him to the door.

"Wait! My phone!" the President exclaimed, as he tried to free himself from the agent's grasp to get to his cell phone.

Agent Walters held firm. "Don't bother, sir. It doesn't work."

The President looked at him in shock. "How do you know it doesn't work?"

"Because none of them work, sir—not yours, mine, or anyone else's, so far."

The President stopped dead in his tracks. "Dear God. Do you know what this could mean?"

Walters prodded him on. "Yes, sir, we're pretty sure we do. They'll meet you in the bunker."

When the President got to the ready room in the bunker, his chief of staff, Vanessa Jackson, was already there. She had on a radio headset attached to a large ham radio-style unit. The ground above them shielded the electronics below. When he walked in the door, he heard the tail end of her conversation.

"Yes, Admiral, let us know as soon as you find out something for sure. We'll be waiting for your call." She took the headset off and handed it to the Navy radio operator seated in front of the unit. She turned to the President.

"Well, what is it, Vanessa? Is it ..."

"Sir, we are still getting reports in, but it looks like we have indeed been hit with an EMP. Everything above ground is knocked out, but we can still communicate with any of the silos, as well as our ships not in port here, and our military bases not in the lower forty-eight. Intelligence is telling us there was confirmation of a missile entering our atmosphere, but before we could launch a counter-attack, it detonated. The altitude was high enough to take out the power grid in the entire continental United States, as well as southern Canada and northern Mexico. The country is dark, sir."

The President stood there in shock, then said only one word. "Who?"

Vanessa shook her head. "Nothing positive on that yet. We only got a short glimpse of the missile before it exploded. However, there is speculation it came from—"

Olstein interrupted her, face dark red. "Russia, right? I knew that asshole was just buttering us up so he could shove a nuke up our—"

"No sir. The trajectory seems to indicate the Korean Peninsula."

Olstein was spluttering. "B-but, we have a base in South Korea! Thirty-five thousand troops! How could they launch a nuclear missile and no one know about it?"

"We're trying to find that out, sir," she replied. "Apparently, they have acquired stealth technology from someone. In the meantime, we need to declare a state of emergency for the entire country, enact martial law, and find as many house members as we can to declare this as an act of war."

"Ha! Good luck with that. They all went home Friday," the President said with a snort.

"I think the Speaker is still here. I've sent a runner over to his residence. He wasn't planning to fly out until Monday." Vanessa was checking some paperwork she had apparently brought with her. She looked pointedly at him. "Some of the joint chiefs may be in town. However, you don't need any of them or their approval to act right now."

Olstein returned her gaze then changed his focus to a pen stand on the desk. "We can't attack anybody until we know who did this, Vanessa. We have to know for sure … be one hundred percent positive. I mean, none of our bases will be at full capacity. They have no way of calling the troops in. All hell is going to break loose here. We'll need to recall all of our troops to maintain law and order in this country. We won't have the manpower to launch an attack."

Vanessa rolled her eyes. He wasn't looking at her anyway. *Spineless, as always,* she thought. She said aloud, "Sir, those are valid points, but we cannot appear weak in the eyes of the world. You *know* who's responsible! It *has* to be North Korea! If this attack goes unanswered, every piss-ant country over there will be looking to come here and get their licks in as well."

"Exactly! That's why we can't afford to go looking for a fight. We'll need our troops here, protecting us," he replied defensively.

Exasperated, she barked out, "We don't have to look for a fight—we're in one! We've been attacked! Do you think the American people expect you to just sit here and protect your own ass?"

"How dare you talk to me like that! I'm the President of the United States! I'm the Commander in Chief! I decide what our military will do and where they will do it! We are bringing our troops home to protect all the people in our country, not just me or the Capitol! Get me every top military member we can find. I want all of them back here, *now*!" He stormed out of the room to his sleeping quarters.

With a heavy sigh, Vanessa called her executive assistant, David Strain, in. "David, we need to get in touch with every senior military officer we can find in D.C. You may have to go door to door, since we have no cell service or landlines."

David had a confused look on his face. "Um, how are we going to get there? Every modern vehicle up there is incapacitated."

"Damn. I forgot. One sec." She went to the radio operator. "Get me General Everley. Tell him we need at least four Humvees from the hardened storage over here immediately. Also, tell him the president wants all of our deployed troops back ASAP. When he raises hell about bringing our troops home, patch him through to the president. His idea, he can explain it." She turned back to David. "As soon as the Humvees get here, start trying to find the senior staff and get them down here. The shit storm up above may be mild compared to what is going to go down when they get here."

Acknowledgments

Hello friends. I'm so glad to be able to bring you this next series, Perilous Miles. As a prepper, even if you're just starting out or well-seasoned, you know people who don't get it. They call you their crazy prepper friend, their tinfoil hat-wearing buddy ... you get the gist. They go through life living in the moment, don't know how to cook real food (or don't care to), and have no clue how to live without technology. That's where this story came from. I know a lot of them. I often wonder how they would fare if the shit ever did hit the fan. I don't think most of them would make it. We'll see if Carly, Will, and the rest of their family do.

Since I'm self-publishing again, I am back to my original cast of characters in my work. First, as usual, is my husband, Jim. I quit my job to write full-time this year and, while I was terrified, he was thrilled. He is always there for me to bounce scenarios off; he does the covers; he gives me all the time my muse needs–whenever, wherever. He came up with the series title for me. He is my biggest fan, and I couldn't do this without him and his support. Thank you, Baby.

Next is my aunt, Carol. She helps me keep the commas in the right spots and the grammar correct. She has a fulltime job raising her two grandchildren, yet drops everything to work on my books and I love her for it. If you need a proofreader/editor, I can hook you up with her. Thank you, sweet aunt.

My dad is always there if I need to ask technical questions about how things work, especially older items that might still function in an EMP situation. He's a smart man with years of experience in lots of different areas. He tells me when my imagined scenario isn't quite feasible and lets me go down the path anyway when I stubbornly leave it in. I think that's because he sees himself in that stubborn streak. I made a huge change in mine and Jim's lives when I quit my "real" job to write fulltime. I thought he might be disappointed in me for taking that chance. He was one hundred percent behind me. Thanks for having my back, Dad.

Any of you who follow my Facebook page know I lost my mom in January 2017. I inherited so many things from her: my love of music, my skill with numbers, my obsession with puzzles, and one of my most prized attributes–my love of reading. That one is the one that led me down the path I'm on now. I'm sad that she isn't here to share this journey with me, but I know she's watching from above, encouraging me to see how far I can go. I love you, Mom. I miss you every day. Thank you.

Last, and most important, I give the glory to God that He blessed me with this gift to tell stories people want to read. I placed my life in His hands and all I have is because of Him. Thank you, Lord, for the many blessings you bestow upon me every day.

~~~~~

Book 2 in the Perilous Miles series, 15 Miles from Home, should be available in the spring. Stay tuned!

Find P.A. Glaspy on the web!

http://paglaspy.com/ – the website, always updating, so keep coming back for more info. Want to stay up to date on all our latest news? Join our mailing list for updates, giveaways, and events! You'll find a spot to sign up on the right side of the website. We don't spam, ever.

https://www.facebook.com/paglaspy/ – Facebook Fan Page

https://twitter.com/paglaspy – Follow on Twitter

https://www.amazon.com/P.A.-Glaspy/e/B01H131TOE/ref=sr_tc_2_0?qid=1475525227&sr=8-2-ent – Amazon Author Page

https://www.goodreads.com/author/show/15338867.P_A_GLASPY – Goodreads Author Page

https://www.bookbub.com/authors/p-a-glaspy – BookBub Author Page

23513166R00048

Made in the USA
Columbia, SC
09 August 2018